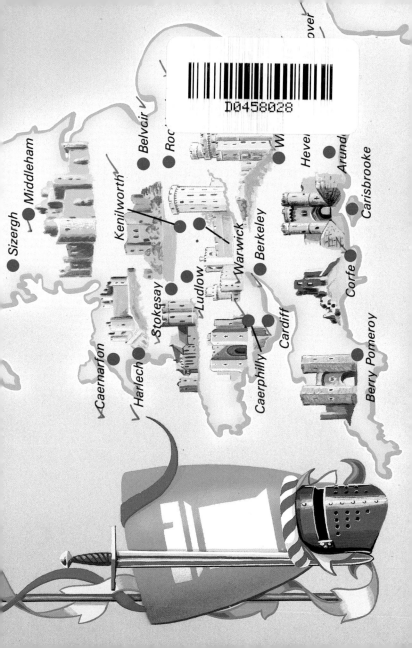

Sizergh

Middleham

Belvoir

Roc...

W...

Hever

Arund...

Carisbrooke

Kenilworth

Warwick

Berkeley

Corfe

Caernarfon

Harlech

Stokesay

Ludlow

Cardiff

Caerphilly

Berry Pomeroy

# CONTENTS

*Cover:* Bodiam Castle   *Back cover:* The Great Hall,
Warwick Castle   *Title page:* Windsor Castle

*Acknowledgments*
The front endpaper map and illustrations on pages 5, 13 and 38 are by
Robin Davies. Photographs are reproduced by courtesy of:
Aerofilms Ltd, pages 8, 15, 22, 32, 41, 42, 46; Ms Judy Appelbee,
page 47 (bottom); Arundel Castle Trustees, pages 44 (2) and 45 (2);
Britain on View, front cover, title page and pages 6, 7 (bottom), 10 (2),
12, 14, 16/17, 20, 24, 25 (2), 35, 36 (2), 37 (top), 43 (middle and
bottom); Mr Chris Bryan, page 40; Cardiff City Council, page 7 (top);
English Heritage, pages 38 and 39 (2); English Life Publications,
pages 28 (2) and 29; Fotomas Index, page 4; Mr Andrew Graham,
pages 46 and 47; Paul Hamlyn Publishing/Country Life Books, page 51;
Heart of England Tourist Board, pages 21 (2) and 23; Hever Castle,
page 37; Leeds Castle, page 43 (top); Dr Ian Morrison, pages 48 and 49;
the National Trust, pages 26 and 33 (2); Photo Source, pages 9 and
34/35; Raby Castle, pages 30 (2) and 31 (2); Scottish Tourist Board,
pages 50/51; Warwick Castle Ltd (John Wright Photography), back
cover and pages 18 (2) and 19.
*Designed by* Graham Marlow.

British Library Cataloguing in Publication Data

Wright, Elizabeth
    Castles.
    1. Great Britain. Castles – For children
    I. Title
    941

    ISBN 0-7214-1090-1

First edition

Published by Ladybird Books Ltd  Loughborough  Leicestershire  UK
Ladybird Books Inc  Lewiston  Maine  04240  USA

Printed in England

# DISCOVERING
# Castles

by ELIZABETH WRIGHT

Ladybird Books

## Introduction

In Britain today there are hundreds of castles to discover. Some are superb examples of military architecture, with great towers and battlements, drawbridges and moats. Others are little more than picturesque ruins, heaps of tumbledown stones.

Building a motte-and-bailey castle at Hastings in the days of William the Conqueror – a detail from the Bayeux Tapestry, embroidered in the 11th century

Castles were introduced into England by William the Conqueror. After he had defeated the English at the battle of Hastings in 1066 and declared himself King of England, he built a network of castles all over the country. They were bases from which he and his Norman barons could rule the native people.

The first castles were simple wooden *motte-and-bailey* constructions. Each consisted of a tower built on a *motte* (mound of earth) linked to a *bailey* (an area of land within an outer wall). As many as three thousand were built, but nothing of them now survives except for the outlines of their earthworks in the ground. These can be seen very clearly in aerial photographs.

Later, many of the wooden castles were rebuilt in stone. At any one time the king had upwards of a hundred royal castles, which in his absence were in the charge of an officer called a Constable. There were also about five hundred baronial castles, built with the king's permission, by noblemen that he trusted.

*A typical motte-and-bailey castle*

A castle had two functions: military and domestic. It could be described as a fortified home – or as a residential fortress. For as well as extensive fortifications, it would also have elaborate apartments for the lord and his family.

By the eighteenth century castles were neither needed nor, since the introduction of cannon, useful. In the nineteenth century, it became fashionable to build stately homes as 'pretend' medieval castles. These castles had no military purpose, but were very grand and richly decorated. The Marquis of Bute's castle at Cardiff, for example, has an Arab Room with a stalactite ceiling of marble and cedar and a banqueting hall with a roof supported by elaborately carved angels.

*Banqueting hall in Cardiff Castle*

Within the grounds of the nineteenth century castle is the simple Norman *shell keep* (an open tower) giving a strong contrast to the later mock Gothic castle.

No two medieval castles were built alike. Even those built to a similar plan would have different layouts to fool any attacker. This, together with the fact that castles reflect so much of the country's history, makes them fascinating buildings to explore.

*Window at Cardiff Castle showing King Henry VII and his queen, Elizabeth of York*

## Windsor Castle

Windsor is the largest inhabited castle in the world, on a site overlooking the Thames in Berkshire.

Windsor is a *linear* castle. This means that it was built as a chain or *line* of baileys (enclosed courtyards) along a ridge of high land.

William the Conqueror built the first timber motte-and-bailey castle at Windsor in 1067. It was one of a ring of castles a day's march from London, and from each other, to protect his newly won capital. The first stone buildings, including the Round Tower, were begun under

*Windsor is one of the Queen's three official residences – together with Buckingham Palace in London and Holyroodhouse in Edinburgh – and is the only castle to have been used as a royal home for the past five hundred years*

*St George's Chapel, Windsor*

Henry II. Later monarchs have all added to the castle – for example, Henry VIII built the main entrance gate. In the nineteenth century, in the reign of George IV, the castle was remodelled into the imposing royal palace that it is today.

In the Middle Ages hunting was the 'sport of kings'. There was so much game in the nearby forests that Windsor soon became a favourite royal hunting lodge.

In 1348 Edward III founded the Order of the Knights of the Garter, the highest order of chivalry in England, at Windsor. You can see the banners of today's Garter Knights in the Chapel of St George, a beautiful Gothic building with a magnificent fan-vaulted ceiling.

Elizabeth I and her Court were often at Windsor. At the queen's command, Shakespeare wrote the comedy *The Merry Wives of Windsor* to entertain them.

During the Civil War, Windsor was held by the Parliamentarians and so was never damaged by siege. Charles I was held prisoner at Windsor before his trial and execution, and he is also buried there.

The castle has fabulous collections of paintings, tapestries, arms and armour, books and furniture, many of which you can see.

## Dover Castle

Built high on the White Cliffs above the English Channel, Dover Castle in Kent is one of the greatest medieval fortresses in Europe.

*Outward sloping walls form part of the defence*

Henry II's keep forms the hub of the castle. An enormous stone cube – the base is 30 m × 30 m (98 ft × 98 ft) and the walls are almost as high at 29 m (95 ft) – it has square towers in each corner. The walls are 6.5 m (21 ft) thick and have rooms built inside them. At the base of the keep the walls slope *outwards* to make it more difficult to mine underneath.

*Dover Castle*

Surrounding the keep is a *curtain wall* with ten flanking towers and two twin-towered gatehouses.

More defences, including another outer curtain wall and the massive Constable's Gate, were built after Prince Louis of France and his army successfully mined under the northern gatehouse during the reign of King John. Later, Henry VIII added gun bastions, and during the Napoleonic Wars the tops were taken off some of the towers to convert them into artillery platforms.

Dover has always been the 'Key to England' and of great strategic importance in time of war. The castle was further strengthened during the Second World War. Dover Castle still had a military garrison until very recently.

Today, if you visit the castle, you can climb up the great spiral staircases to the top of the keep for a bird's eye view of the fortifications. You can look at the network of tunnels under the castle and see in the huge basement kitchens the trapdoors in the ceilings through which food was hoisted up to the rooms above. There are also many rooms to be seen, including the 'royal' bedroom with its own *garderobe* (lavatory) in the wall, and the banqueting hall with its display of armour.

### Harlech Castle

Harlech Castle in Gwynedd, North Wales, stands on a rock 61 m (200 ft) above the sea. Silhouetted against the sky and the distant mountain range of Snowdonia, its massive ramparts and drum towers make it one of the most spectacular castles in Britain.

*Harlech Castle*

Begun in 1283 during Edward I's military campaign in Wales, it was one of the links in the king's plan to build an 'iron ring' of castles to encircle the Welsh who were fighting against him and bring them under the power of the English Crown.

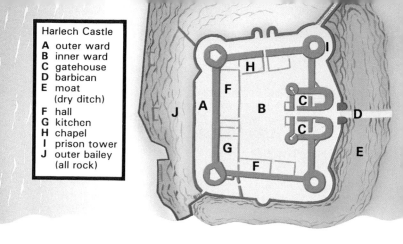

**Harlech Castle**

A outer ward
B inner ward
C gatehouse
D barbican
E moat (dry ditch)
F hall
G kitchen
H chapel
I prison tower
J outer bailey (all rock)

Harlech is a *concentric* – or double – castle, one built within the other. The concentric castle is very hard to attack but can be defended by only a few men.

The castle took six years to complete, and hundreds of men were brought from all over England to work on it. Some of the walls – for example, the twin-towered gatehouse – were 4 m (12 ft) thick. As well as being guarded by a drawbridge, the entrance had three enormous doors and three portcullises – huge iron shutters that slid up and down.

On the seaward side of the castle, a staircase was cut into the rock so that under land siege food could be brought by ship, and the defenders would not be starved into surrender.

Although the outer walls are now mostly in ruins, the castle has survived a great many attacks. Sometimes it has been held by the Welsh, sometimes by the English. In 1468, during the Wars of the Roses, Dafydd ap Einion held the castle and his exploits are still remembered in the song 'Men of Harlech'.

### Caerphilly Castle

Caerphilly is the largest castle in Wales and in Britain it is second only to Windsor in size.

Gilbert de Clare, Lord of Glamorgan, began building it in 1268 to protect his lands from the Welsh. But the castle was only half finished when Llywelyn ap Gruffydd, the last native Prince of Wales, knocked it down and Gilbert had to start all over again.

The finished castle was magnificent. Surrounded by moats (ditches filled with water), artificial lakes and a screen wall or dam 305 m (1000 ft) long, Caerphilly had the most complex water defences of any castle in Britain. A concentric castle, with circles of defences each greater than the last for the attacker to scale, it could not be taken by any of the usual methods of siege warfare – scaling ladders, stone-firing catapults or tunnelling under the walls.

After the Civil War the walls were *slighted* – deliberately destroyed – and the castle fell into decay. It was restored during the last century, but still has a ruined tower that leans outwards, defying the laws of gravity.

*This aerial view shows how strong the water defences were at Caerphilly Castle*

**Caernarfon Castle**

In Welsh, Caernarfon means 'fort on the shore'. The Romans built the first fort, giving Caernarfon its name, but the present castle was built by Edward I during his military campaigns against the Welsh.

Edward intended Caernarfon to be the centre of English rule in Wales. As well as being a great military fortress, Caernarfon was to have suites of royal apartments for the king and his court. The first English Prince of Wales

– the future Edward II – was indeed born here in 1284, but within ten years the castle had been captured and sacked by the Welsh in the Madog rebellion.

Siege and repeated attacks, neglect, and the ravages of time and weather eventually reduced the castle to a roofless shell. In the nineteenth century it was restored, and in this century it has become a magnificent setting for the Investiture of the Prince of Wales. Prince Charles was invested here as Prince of Wales in 1969.

## Warwick Castle

The great curtain walls and the high towers flanking its massive gatehouse make Warwick one of the most picturesque of medieval castles.

*The dungeon at Warwick*

William I built the first castle at Warwick in 1068. It was to safeguard his march to York to force the northern English earls to accept Norman rule. This castle was completely rebuilt in the fourteenth century by Thomas Beauchamp, turning it into the fortified great house that exists today.

In the rebuilding a great deal of attention was paid to the living quarters as well as to the castle's defences, and a magnificent Great Hall 19 m (62 ft) long was made. Later owners continued to make the residential apartments more beautiful with cedarwood panelling, marble Adam fireplaces, Aubusson carpets and crystal chandeliers.

*The Great Hall, Warwick Castle*

## Kenilworth Castle

Kenilworth Castle in Warwickshire was built in the twelfth century by Geoffrey de Clinton, Treasurer to Henry I. Although the castle is now largely in ruins, it was once such a formidable stronghold that King John was made to surrender it when he signed Magna Carta in 1215.

John of Gaunt inherited Kenilworth through his wife, Blanche. He built a magnificent Great Hall and considerably extended the private apartments.

Henry IV inherited the castle from his father, John of Gaunt, and it remained a royal castle until 1563, when Elizabeth I gave it to the Earl of Leicester, her favourite and one of her suitors.

Kenilworth Castle has a romantic place in history, because the Earl of Leicester entertained Queen Elizabeth here. Two hundred and fifty years later, Sir Walter Scott's historical novel, *Kenilworth*, made the castle famous once more.

## Ludlow Castle

*Ludlow Castle from the river*

Ludlow Castle in Shropshire was built in 1085 by Roger de Lacy, a Norman knight. Because of its position on the Welsh March – or Border – it has always been an important stronghold, and it later became the residence of the Lords President of the Council of Wales.

During the Wars of the Roses Ludlow supported the Yorkists, and it was from here that the young Edward V set out with his brother for his coronation in London – only to be imprisoned in the Tower of London and eventually to die there. The tower where the young princes had lived at Ludlow thereafter became known as the Princes' Tower.

It was at Ludlow Castle in 1634 that John Milton's masque *Comus* – a glittering spectacle of music, poetry and pageant – was first performed by the Countess of Shrewsbury's children, and plays are still staged here today as part of the Ludlow Festival.

*The ramparts at Ludlow Castle*

## Stokesay Castle

Stokesay, a fortified manor house in Shropshire, is a unique medieval survival. It still has the kind of domestic interior that was once common in larger castles but which later owners swept away as they modernised them into grander, more luxurious palaces.

Originally owned by the de Say family, Stokesay was bought in 1281 by Laurence de Ludlow, a wealthy wool merchant. He built the Great Hall, with its fine timbered roof and central hearth. Above the hall was a *solar* – the family's private sitting room. It was entered by an outside staircase and so cut off from the hall, although the family could watch what was going on below through the 'squint' holes on either side of the solar's fireplace.

Ten years later, Laurence was given a licence by Edward I to fortify his manor house, and he built the south tower. Stokesay is a strange mixture of military and domestic architecture – the lower part of the north tower has narrow, pointed lancet windows, while the half timbered, projecting upper storey has unusually large windows for a thirteenth century fortified house.

### Berkeley Castle

Berkeley (pronounced Bark-li) Castle in Gloucestershire was given by Henry II to his supporter, Robert Fitzharding, in 1153, and it has been owned and lived in by his descendants ever since.

Apart from the twelfth century keep, most of the buildings date from the fourteenth century, when the castle was completely rebuilt.

Tradition suggests that the castle was rebuilt to hide the evidence of a crime against the state. For King Edward II was murdered here in 1327 on the orders of his wife, Queen Isabella, and her lover, the Earl Mortimer. At first the king had been imprisoned in a room above the castle's cesspit, in the hope that the fumes would make him ill. When this failed, the king was savagely killed.

*The Great Hall at Berkeley*

Today, Berkeley is a beautifully preserved castle, including a fourteenth century Great Hall with a saddle-beam timber roof and the famous five sided 'Berkeley arches'. It also has a chapel whose wooden roof is painted with texts from the Book of Revelations. In the castle grounds there is an Elizabethan garden and an ancient bowling alley.

*Sir Francis Drake's sea chest*

## Corfe Castle

Overlooking a break in the Purbeck hills in Dorset, Corfe Castle takes its name from the old English word *corfe* meaning 'gap' or 'pass'. Although it now lies in ruins, it was once one of the strongest castles in England and was never taken by assault.

William I built the first stone castle where earlier Saxon kings had once had a hunting lodge. The twin-towered gateway became known as the Martyr's Gate, for it was built on the place where young King Edward the Martyr had been murdered on the orders of his stepmother Elfrida so that her son, Ethelred the Unready, could succeed to the throne.

Corfe Castle was the scene of many more dark deeds. William I's son, Robert, Duke of Normandy, was imprisoned here, as was King John's wife, and later Edward II. At Corfe, King John starved to death twenty two French nobles for supporting the claim of his nephew Arthur to the crown.

In 1571 Elizabeth I sold it to Sir Christopher Hatton, one of her courtiers, and so it was no longer a royal castle. It remained a royalist castle, however, and during the Civil War, Lady Bankes, wife of the Lord Chief Justice, held it for the king. Corfe resisted the Roundheads' siege for a record nineteen months and only fell through the treachery of a member of the garrison. As a punishment, Parliament ordered the walls to be slighted and the castle was reduced to ruins.

*Alnwick Castle*

*The stone defenders of Alnwick Castle*

## Alnwick Castle

Although much restored in the nineteenth century, Alnwick (pronounced *Annick*) Castle dominates the Northumbrian countryside just as it did in the Middle Ages. The battlements of the barbican – the tower built to protect the main gateway of a castle – are still manned by stone warriors, decoy targets to fool besieging marksmen. From a distance they look deceptively lifelike.

*The Library, Alnwick Castle*

During the time of the fiercest Border warfare between the Scots and the English, Alnwick was the stronghold of the Percy family. They were descendants of William de Percy, a Norman knight who had come to England with William the Conqueror. The Percys led many raids into Scotland from Alnwick, and in turn had to defend themselves against Scottish attacks. Many prisoners have languished in Alnwick's *donjon*, or keep, including King William 'The Lion' of Scotland, who in 1174 was unwise enough to ride too close to the castle one foggy morning.

Today, Alnwick is a magnificent country house, the home of the Duke of Northumberland.

*Raby Castle*

## Raby Castle

Raby Castle in County Durham was the medieval stronghold of the Nevills, one of the most powerful families in the north of England. Built around a

*The drawing room, Raby Castle*

rectangular courtyard, the castle has a long battlemented front and nine distinctive towers, each with its own name – Clifford's, Joan's, Kitchen, Bulmer's, Watch, Chapel, Mount Raskelf, Keep and Nevill Gateway.

In 1569, the northern earls plotted in Raby's vast Barons' Hall to put Mary Queen of Scots on the throne of England. When the Rising of the North failed and the power of the Nevills was destroyed, Raby was forfeited to the Crown and eventually became the property of the Vanes.

*The Barons' Hall, Raby*

*The 14th century Great Kitchen*

Today, Raby is a great country house within the old medieval walls. It has a superb octagonal (eight sided) Victorian drawing room and a Gothic-style entrance hall with dark red pillars.

## Middleham Castle

The once great but now ruined castle of Middleham in North Yorkshire had the largest *keep* (the strongest place in a castle) in England. Built in 1170 by Robert Fitz-Ralph, the keep still stands, together with the thirteenth century chapel, the entrance to the gatehouse and the curtain walls.

In the thirteenth century Middleham came through marriage into the hands of the powerful Nevills.

In 1646 after the Civil War, the fortifications of Middleham Castle were dismantled. No longer needed as a fortress, it was never adapted for purely domestic purposes and fell into decay and ruin.

## Sizergh Castle

*The Pele Tower, Sizergh Castle*

Sizergh Castle in Cumbria was built as a pele tower in the fourteenth century. To protect themselves against reivers (armed bands of robbers) in those turbulent and lawless times, families on both sides of the Border began to build fortified tower houses, or pele towers, to live in. Usually, the tower stood within a *barmkin* or fortified courtyard.

By Tudor times, life was more secure and comfortable, and Sizergh became a fine country house, with plasterwork ceilings, panelled walls and elaborate overmantels for the fireplaces.

Sizergh Castle was owned by the Strickland family for seven hundred years, and now belongs to the National Trust.

*The Queen's room, Sizergh*

### Bodiam Castle

Bodiam Castle in East Sussex was built in 1385 as a
defence against a threatened French invasion.

Built round an inner courtyard, the castle has drum
towers in each corner and square towers in the middle of
each of the high outer walls with arrow slits for archers.
In the ceiling of the gatehouse you can see *murder holes*,
which were made so that boiling oil, tar or water could
be poured on anyone who managed to break through the
outer gate.

Inside, hardly anything is left of the rooms round the
courtyard, for much of the castle was destroyed when it
was slighted in the seventeenth century by the
Parliamentarians after the Civil War in 1642-6.

But there is a room in the northwest tower which still has a fireplace and garderobe in the wall, and you can visit this from the rampart walk.

Bodiam is surrounded by a moat as large as a lake, where swans sail serenely among the water lilies. Seen today in summer sunlight, Bodiam looks like a fairytale castle floating on the reflection of its own towers and battlements.

*Bodiam – a fairytale castle floating on its own reflection*

## Hever Castle

Hever Castle in Kent was built in the thirteenth century as a fortified farmhouse, surrounded by a moat and with a wooden drawbridge. By the fifteenth century it was a prosperous manor house and its owners were given royal permission to *crenellate*, that is, to add stone battlements to its walls.

Hever was the childhood home of Anne Boleyn, and it was here that Henry VIII came to court his second wife. For a brief time Hever became famous – and then notorious as the queen fell from favour and was beheaded in 1536 on Tower Green.

*The gatehouse at Hever – Note the gun loops (upside-down keyholes through which cannon could be fired)*

When Anne's father died a year after her execution, Hever became crown property. In 1540 Henry VIII gave

it to Anne of Cleves, his fourth wife, whom he had recently divorced. Hever, a little moated manor house, has therefore been home to two tragic queens of England.

*Inside the gatehouse – the winch for the drawbridge is on the left*

Later, Hever became a house of call for smugglers coming up from the coast. Beef, beer, and bread and cheese would be left on the table in the Great Hall, and in return for Hever's open doors a keg of brandy or tobacco would be there in the morning.

When the American millionaire William Waldorf Astor bought Hever in 1903, ducks and geese swam on the old moat, for it had long since become a simple farmhouse once more. Now beautifully restored, Hever Castle has a fine collection of armour, superb tapestries and paintings.

*The Loggia – part of Hever's beautiful gardens*

## Carisbrooke Castle

Carisbrooke was first a Roman fort, then a medieval castle, and finally an Elizabethan artillery battery. In appearance it looks medieval, although some of the Roman walling still survives, and the Elizabethan artillery ramparts completely encircle the castle.

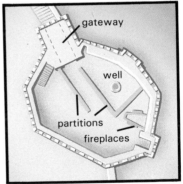

*The shell keep, Carisbrooke Castle*

Because of its position on the Isle of Wight, Carisbrooke has often been attacked by French raiders, but without success. In the years before the Armada, fear of a Spanish attack led to the strengthening of its defences with cannon.

After the Civil War, Charles I was imprisoned in Carisbrooke Castle after his escape from Hampton Court in 1647.

One of Carisbrooke's attractions today is the sixteenth century well house (the well itself was sunk in 1150) where a donkey is still used to haul up the water.

*The Great Staircase*

39

## Berry Pomeroy Castle

Berry Pomeroy Castle in Devon now lies in ruins,
haunted by ghosts. It was built in 1300 by Ralph de
Pomeroy and his twin-towered gatehouse still stands. It
remained in his family until it was sold in 1548 to
Edward Seymour, Lord Protector of England and the
most powerful man in the land. Later, in 1600, the
Seymour family built a great Tudor mansion within the
walls of the old medieval castle and decorated it lavishly
with marble and alabaster and fine panelling.

In 1688 William of Orange and his army landed in
Devon, and the Prince stayed at Berry Pomeroy before
beginning his march on London. Twelve years later, this
great mansion was mysteriously destroyed by fire. How
it happened no one knows, for there is no record of the
event other than the comment of the local vicar, John
Prince, in his *Worthies of Devon* – 'all this Glory lieth
in the Dust, buried in its own Ruines'.

Many ghosts haunt this Devonshire castle. One is Henry de Pomeroy, who killed a herald and then stabbed himself to death. Another is Margaret de Pomeroy, who was locked up and starved to death by her sister for falling in love with the same knight as herself.

However, Berry Pomeroy does have some happier traditions, including a wishing tree in the castle grounds that is supposed to grant the wishes of anyone who walks round it backwards three times.

### Rockingham Castle

Rockingham in Northamptonshire was a royal castle of the Norman kings of England. It was a particular favourite with King John, who used it as a hunting lodge when chasing deer in the nearby forest.

Little remains of the medieval castle except for the two powerful D-shaped towers of the gatehouse, built by Edward I. By 1530 it had fallen into decay.

Edward Watson, an ancestor of the present owners, leased and then bought it from the Crown and built a fine Tudor mansion on the site of the medieval bailey (or courtyard). One of the attractions of the house today is the approach through the servants' quarters, along a cobbled street of old bakehouses and breweries.

The writer Charles Dickens often stayed here and he used the house as a model for Chesney Wold, the great country mansion in *Bleak House*.

*Henry VIII banqueting hall*

*Lady Baillie's bedroom*

## Leeds Castle

Leeds in Kent is a beautiful moated medieval castle dating from the twelfth century, although much restored in more modern times. It stands on two islands in an artificial lake, and a magnificent two tiered enclosed bridge connects the main building to the keep.

Leeds became known as the 'Lady's Castle' because of the many queens of England who have lived here, including Catherine of Aragon and Elizabeth I.

## Arundel Castle

Arundel in West Sussex is a medieval castle restored in the nineteenth century. It is the home of the Duke of Norfolk, the premier Duke of England and hereditary Earl Marshal, who presides over the College of Arms.

The oldest part of Arundel, the eleventh century shell keep, stands on a grassy mound 21 m (70 ft) high, the motte of an earlier castle. Much of Arundel's later medieval fortifications were destroyed by cannon in 1643 during the Civil War, but have been rebuilt.

*The Picture Gallery, Arundel*

Superb Victorian craftsmanship can be seen in the remodelled interior, including the great hall, grand staircase and the state apartments.

Among the many fine things on display is the homage throne from Queen Victoria's coronation. Queen Victoria herself visited the castle in 1846. Before her arrival, the 13th Duke of Norfolk had a stained-glass window showing the Biblical scene of Solomon entertaining the Queen of Sheba removed from the dining room, since he feared it would not meet with royal approval.

*The Dining Room*

*The Victoria Room*

*Although the present-day Belvoir Castle is not of great age, a Norman castle once stood on its commanding site*

### Belvoir Castle

Belvoir (pronounced *Beever*) Castle in Leicestershire is a romantic Regency fantasy built in mock-medieval Gothic style in the early nineteenth century.

Displays of jousting – contests on horseback between armed knights at a tournament conducted according to the rules of medieval chivalry – take place regularly in the grounds today.

## Balmoral Castle

Balmoral Castle on Deeside in Grampian is the summer home of the Queen and the Royal Family. It was built in 1853 for Queen Victoria and Prince Albert in Scottish Baronial style – the Victorian ideal of what a medieval castle should look like.

Queen Victoria had first rented and then bought the original fifteenth century castle as a summer holiday home before deciding to build a new castle. The old castle had been called Bouchmorale – an appropriate name since in Gaelic it means 'majestic dwelling'.

*The Queen and the Duke of Edinburgh relaxing at Balmoral*

**Edinburgh Castle**

Edinburgh Castle stands high on a rock 82 m (270 ft) above the city. A natural fortress, the rock – an extinct volcano – has been fortified since the Bronze Age.

The castle's history is the history of Scotland, for it was the centre of conflicts between kings and their nobles, and the prize fought for in the wars between the Scots and the English. To hold Edinburgh Castle was to hold Scotland.

The oldest building in the castle is the tiny eleventh century St Margaret's Chapel. In 1313, when the Earl of Moray and his men daringly scaled the south face of the rock to seize the castle from the English, the earl carried out the orders of the king, Robert I (Robert Bruce), and destroyed all the fortifications and buildings except for the chapel.

Edinburgh Castle was both a refuge and prison for James II of Scotland, who came to the throne while still a boy after the murder of his father. In 1440, despite the pleas and tears of the nine year old king, the young Earl of Douglas was dragged by his enemies, jealous of the royal friendship, from a banquet in the castle and murdered on the Castlehill. Thereafter the banquet became known as the 'Black Dinner' –

> 'Edinburgh Castle, toun and toure
> God grant thou sink for sinne
> An' that even for the black dinner
> Earl Douglas gat therein.'

King James VI of Scotland and I of England was born in the castle's royal apartments, where the 'Honours of Scotland' – the crown, sword and sceptre of the Scottish kings – are now kept.

In 1745 Bonnie Prince Charlie and his Highlanders besieged and took the castle during the Jacobite Rebellion. This was the last time the castle came under attack.

Today, the castle is famous for its military tattoo which takes place every year on the Esplanade in front of the castle during the Edinburgh Festival.

## Glamis Castle

Glamis (pronounced *Glahms*) in Angus was once a
hunting lodge of the kings of Scotland. In 1372 Robert
II gave it to his Keeper of the Privy Seal, Sir John Lyon,
who later married the king's daughter. Sir John
completely rebuilt the lodge as a battlemented tower
house.

During the seventeenth century Glamis was embellished
with conical turrets in the style of a French *château* or
castle. The medieval fortress was remodelled, the great
hall becoming the drawing room, with its stone vault
covered by a plasterwork ceiling. The dungeon became a
wine cellar.

According to Shakespeare, Macbeth lived at Glamis, but there is no historical record to support this claim.

The Old Chevalier, the father of Bonnie Prince Charlie, stayed at Glamis before his unsuccessful attempt to regain the throne for the Stuart kings in the first Jacobite Rising in 1716.

Glamis, too, has many modern associations with royalty, for it was the childhood home of the Queen Mother. Visitors can still see today the Royal Suite of rooms that she and George VI, then Duke of York, used in the 1920s. In 1930 Princess Margaret was born at Glamis Castle.

*The Queen Mother's sitting room at Glamis*

# Glossary

**bailey**  An enclosed area or courtyard within the castle.

**barbican**  A tower built to protect the main gate of a castle.

**barmkin**  Fortified courtyard.

**concentric castle**  A castle built within the circle of another castle – the opposite of *linear* construction.

**crenellate**  To add stone battlements to walls.

**curtain wall**  High outer wall of a castle.

**donjon**  The *keep*, the strongest place in the castle. Prisoners were often kept here and the word *dungeon* developed from it, but at first it meant simply the strongest – and safest – place in the castle.

**drawbridge**  Wooden bridge across a *moat*. It could be raised to make the castle more secure.

**garderobe**  A French word meaning 'protect your clothes' which described a primitive lavatory built over a drain shaft in the castle wall.

**keep**  The strongest place – usually a tower – in a castle.

**linear castle**  A castle built as a line or chain of enclosed *baileys* – the opposite of *concentric*, where the castle was built as a circle within a circle.

**moat**  A ditch filled with water. It was often made by damming a river, and could be very wide.

**motte**  A high mound, the earthwork defence on which a motte-and-bailey castle was built.

**murder hole**  An opening in the ceiling of a gatehouse through which boiling water, oil, tar and so on could be poured on attackers storming the gatehouse.

**pele tower**  A fortified house built as a tower.

**portcullis**  An entrance gate raised or lowered in grooves.

**shell keep**  An open tower, one of the earliest forms of stone castle.

**slight**  To deliberately destroy fortifications after a castle had been captured. Many royalist castles were slighted by the Parliamentarians after the Civil War (1642-6).

**solar**  The private sitting room in a castle for a lord and his family.

**ward**  A later word for *bailey*.